NOW A BIG MOTION PICTURE

GULLIVER'S TRAVELS

The Tale of Gulliver

by Emily Sollinger

based on the screenplay written by
Joe Stillman and Nicholas Stoller

Ready-to-Read

Simon Spotlight
New York   London   Toronto   Sydney

SIMON SPOTLIGHT

An imprint of Simon & Schuster Children's Publishing Division
1230 Avenue of the Americas, New York, New York 10020
© 2010 Twentieth Century Fox Film Corporation. All Rights Reserved.
Movie photography © 2010 Twentieth Century Fox Film Corporation. All Rights Reserved.
© 2010 iStockphoto/Thinkstock © 2010 Hemera/Thinkstock
All rights reserved, including the right of reproduction in whole
or in part in any form. SIMON SPOTLIGHT, READY-TO-READ, and colophon are
registered trademarks of Simon & Schuster, Inc.
For information about special discounts for bulk purchases, please contact
Simon & Schuster Special Sales at 1-866-506-1949 or business@simonandschuster.com.
Manufactured in the United States of America 1010 LAK
First Edition
2 4 6 8 10 9 7 5 3 1
ISBN 978-1-4424-0866-1

Buzz! Buzz! Buzz! A loud alarm clock sounded in a small apartment in New York City. Lemuel Gulliver got out of bed and jumped into the shower. He quickly dressed, gulped down his coffee, read the newspaper, and headed out the door.

Gulliver finally arrived at his office. He had worked in the mail room of the *New York Tribune* newspaper for ten years. For ten years he'd had a secret crush on the travel editor, Darcy. Gulliver decided today he would ask her out.

Darcy looked up from her desk to find Gulliver staring at her.

"Are you all right?" she asked.

"Sure," he said, chickening out. "I just came in for this," he added, taking a piece of paper from her desk.

"You are applying for the travel-writing assignment?" asked Darcy.

"Exactly," said Gulliver.

"Wow!" Darcy exclaimed. "I had no idea you wrote—or traveled. Bring me some samples, and we'll see what we can do."

But he was not a writer or a traveler. What had he gotten himself into?

After hours of trying to write samples, Gulliver gave up. He wanted to impress Darcy so much that he copied some articles that had already been published and presented them to her as his own. After reading them, Darcy hired him!

She sent him to Bermuda to interview
a man who claimed to have the secret
to the Bermuda Triangle. The Bermuda
Triangle is a mysterious location in the
middle of the Atlantic Ocean where
ships and planes are known to disappear.

Gulliver was greeted in Bermuda by a man named Young Hank. Young Hank took Gulliver to his grandfather, Old Hank. Old Hank was the man who held the secret to the mysterious Bermuda Triangle. He held tightly to a worn-out notebook.

"In here are coordinates only I know. If you go to that exact spot, the mouth of the sea opens wide," he explained. "I have been there. And I have never been the same!"

Gulliver was even more nervous now.

"Let's get you set up with a boat,"
Young Hank said.

He showed Gulliver how to use the boat's
navigation system and saw him off.

On board, Gulliver tried to write. *Splat!* A drop of rain hit the page. He looked up to see he was sailing into a giant storm. He was approaching a huge gushing waterspout. Suddenly Gulliver and his boat were being pulled into the depths of the sea by a strong whirling wave.

A few moments later, Gulliver slowly opened his eyes. . . .

Everything looked blue. A tiny man, six inches tall, was staring at him.

"Beast!" shouted the tiny man. "I am General Edward Edwardian, Commander of Lilliput. I have captured you and must present you to our king. We know you have been helping our enemies, the Blefuscians. You are wearing their color. What say you, beast?"

"AHHHHH!" Gulliver screamed.

There were hundreds of tiny people. And they were tying him to a giant cart!

"Where am I?" asked Gulliver, as the army of tiny people wheeled him away. "This must be a dream. I'm going to close my eyes. When I open them I'll be back in my bed." When he opened his eyes, Gulliver was not at home. "Can someone please tell me where I am?" he begged.

"You are in Lilliput," answered a tiny soldier. "The greatest, grandest land in all the world."

"All hail Lilliput!" shouted a crowd
of tiny people.

General Edward presented Gulliver
to King Theodore.

"From this day forward, you exist only
to serve and obey," he told Gulliver.

"I told you, I'm not a Blefushton!"
Gulliver pleaded as they led him away.
"I don't even know what that is!"

One of the guards led Gulliver into a cave and locked him inside. "In you go, beast," said the guard.

"All this calling me a beast is starting to get to me!" said Gulliver. "I may be a giant here, but that doesn't mean I don't have feelings!"

"I don't think you are a beast," said a young man next to him. "I'm Horatio."

"It's nice to meet you. I'm Gulliver. Why are you here?" Gulliver asked.

"I looked at the princess, and she plans to marry General Edward," he explained.

"You were locked up just for looking at somebody else's girlfriend? That is cold," Gulliver responded.

"I am just a lowly commoner," Horatio mumbled.

"Don't be so down on yourself. You seem like a cool guy," Gulliver said gently.

Before long, General Edward put Gulliver to work. He was working hard, pulling forty plows across a field, when a loud alarm bell rang.

"The Blefuscians are attacking!" called Edward. "To the castle, beast!"

Gulliver carefully made his way through the city, with an angry Edward directing him. When they made it to the castle, a fire was under way.

"Fear not, my darling!" Edward called to the princess. "I will save you!"

At that moment, Gulliver reached out his giant hand toward the princess who was dangerously close to the fire. She stepped into his palm, and he placed her safely out of the fire's reach.

"We need water quickly!" Horatio shouted as Gulliver tried desperately to reach into the burning buildings to save more people.

"Or a me-size oven mitt!" responded Gulliver.

With skill and strength, Gulliver put the fire out and saved the king.

A loud cheer erupted from the crowd.

"Our hero! The beast!" they shouted.

The king thanked Gulliver for rescuing him and his daughter.

"Now I welcome you to Lilliput, not as a servant, but a guest," said the king.

"Sweet," Gulliver replied with a giggle. He was happy to no longer be a servant. Then the king invited Gulliver to a royal banquet.

"I'll come if you free my friend Horatio and allow me to bring him as my guest."

The king agreed.

At the banquet the king explained that for years Lilliputians and Blefuscians had been capturing each other's princess.

"That's awful," said Gulliver.

"Where are you from?" asked the queen.

"Some believe you are from the Island Where We Dare Not Go," the king said.

"No. I'm from the island of Manhattan," he said. And he told them all about it. "It's a democracy," he explained. "Every four years we elect a president."

Everyone assumed Gulliver was the president. He didn't correct them.

"You must have been a noble and victorious president," said the queen.

"I was known as President the Awesome."

"When will you return to your home?"

"Without my boat, I think I'm stuck here," explained Gulliver.

"We are the finest builders in the land," said the king. "We will build you a suitable place to stay."

Soon Gulliver was settled in his new home, and he loved life in Lilliput. He was loved and treated like royalty. He began to write and really enjoyed it.

"I am beginning to love this place more than my own home," Gulliver wrote. After all, in Lilliput he was a hero. He was President the Awesome!

But soon Gulliver got carried away. He told his friends more things that weren't true—like how Darcy was his princess back home.

One day there was a knock at his door.

"I have good news for you," announced Edward. "I have found your ship. You may return home. Like, immediately."

Gulliver felt sad about leaving, but he knew it was time to go home.

Once he set sail, his cell phone started working. He had a lot of messages.

"*Beep!* Gulliver, it's Darcy. Call me as soon as you get this. I know those samples weren't yours. Now I'm going to have to go there and write it myself!"

Gulliver panicked. He could not face Darcy now! He quickly turned the boat around and headed back to Lilliput.

Upon Gulliver's return, the king made him the new general. When Edward learned he had been replaced, he was furious! He decided to get rid of Gulliver. So he left Lilliput and worked with the Blefuscians to build a giant robot beast even bigger than Gulliver! Then he challenged Gulliver to a duel.

"I accept. It is on," said Gulliver. But as soon as the giant robot beast came toward him, Gulliver was terrified.

"I surrender!" shouted Gulliver.

"You are President the Awesome!" said the king. "You can't surrender!"

"No, I'm not. I'm just a mail-room guy. I was afraid to tell you guys the truth because it was so great being a big shot for the first time in my life. I'm sorry I lied," Gulliver cried.

But sorry wasn't enough, and Gulliver was promptly kicked out of Lilliput.

Horatio searched for Gulliver and
begged him to return. He explained that
since he'd gone, Blefuscia had taken over
Lilliput, and Edward had captured Darcy.

"What? She's . . . Darcy's here?"
Gulliver was stunned.

"You saved our princess and our king,"
Horatio said. "We need you. Let's go."

Gulliver found Darcy in the same cave he
had been in. She wanted to leave, but he
told her the Lilliputians needed him.

"You work in the mail room," Darcy said.

"Not today I don't," Gulliver replied.

So Gulliver fought the big robot again. But this time he won! Then he helped the Lilliputians and the Blefuscians agree to stop fighting and live together.

Everyone thanked Gulliver for everything he had done. Then he and Darcy set sail. As their boat left, Darcy leaned in and gave Gulliver a kiss on the cheek.

Six months later . . .

Back at the *New York Tribune* Gulliver was promoted to travel writer. He noticed a new guy working in the mail room.

"Who are you?" Gulliver asked.

"Just the new guy in the mail room."

Gulliver was happy to offer some advice: "*Just* the mail room? All the greats start in the mail room. Keep the dream alive. There are no small jobs. Only small people. Tiny, *tiny*, little people."